KT-231-377

This book belongs to:

....

....

A catalogue record for this book is available from the British Library

Published by Ladybird Books Ltd
80 Strand London WC2R 0RL
A Penguin Company

2 4 6 8 10 9 7 5 3 1

© Ladybird Books Ltd MMV

Endpaper map illustrations by Fred van Deelen

LADYBIRD and the device of a Ladybird are trademarks of Ladybird Books Ltd

All rights reserved. No part of this publication may be reproduced,
stored in a retrieval system, or transmitted in any form or by any means,
electronic, mechanical, photocopying, recording or otherwise,
without the prior consent of the copyright owner.

ISBN-13: 978-1-84422-306-0
ISBN-10: 1-84422-306-X

Printed in China

LADYBIRD TALES

Snow White
and the
Seven Dwarfs

Retold by Vera Southgate M.A., B.Com

with illustrations by Stuart Williams

Once upon a time on a cold winter's day, as the snowflakes were falling softly and swiftly, a Queen sat sewing by her window.

As she sewed, the Queen pricked her finger and three drops of blood fell upon her sewing.

The red of the blood against the white of the snow, framed by the black wood of the window frame, looked so beautiful that she thought, "O, how I wish I could have a child with skin as white as snow, with cheeks as red as blood and with hair as black as ebony!"

Now it happened that some time afterwards, the Queen did have a baby daughter whose skin was as white as snow, whose cheeks were bright red and whose hair was as black as ebony. The Queen called her little girl Snow White.

Unfortunately, soon after her child was born, the Queen died. A year later the King married again.

The new Queen was very beautiful but much too proud of her own beauty.

Often she stood in front of her magic mirror and asked,

"Mirror, mirror, on the wall, who is the fairest of them all?"

The mirror, for it could only speak the truth, always replied,

"Thou, my Queen, art the fairest of them all!"

Meanwhile, Snow White was growing into a beautiful young girl. One day it happened that when the Queen stood in front of her mirror, it said,

"The truth I must speak and I vow, that the child Snow White is more lovely than thou."

When the Queen heard these words, she was angry and jealous. Hatred for Snow White filled the Queen's heart. She commanded a huntsman to take Snow White into the forest and kill her.

The huntsman led Snow White deep into the forest. When he stopped and drew out his knife to kill her, the poor child wept and begged him to spare her life. "Please do not kill me," she pleaded.

When the huntsman saw the tears on such a young and beautiful face, he took pity on her. He put away his knife and let her go free.

Snow White ran off into the great forest. She did not know which way to go, nor yet what would happen to her. She heard the roars of wild animals and she ran on and on. By evening, her feet were sore, her clothes were torn and her arms and legs were scratched.

Just as Snow White was ready to fall down with weariness, she came to a little cottage. She knocked on the door. There was no reply. She tried the door and it opened, so she went inside to rest.

Everything inside the cottage was small and neat. Against the wall stood seven little beds, each covered with a white bedspread.

Snow White was tired and longing to sleep. She tried six little beds but none suited her until she came to the seventh, which felt just right. She lay down and soon she was fast asleep.

Now the cottage belonged to seven dwarfs who had spent all day in the mountains, digging for gold. As they entered their cottage that evening, they noticed that their beds were not as neat as when they had left them.

"Look who's in my bed!" the seventh dwarf called to the others. The dwarfs stood around the bed together and gazed at the beautiful girl, sleeping soundly. As the dwarfs were anxious not to waken Snow White, they tiptoed away and ate their suppers very quietly.

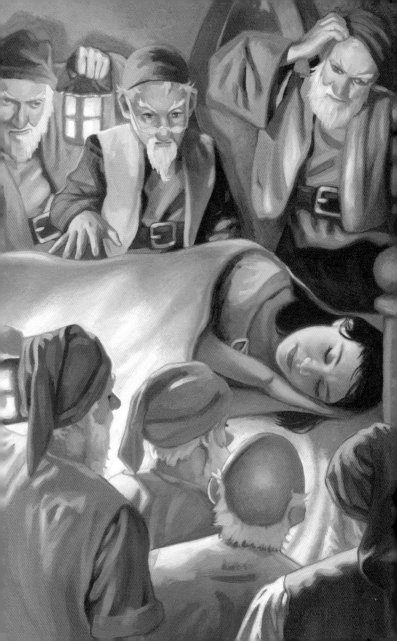

In the morning, when Snow White first awoke and saw the seven dwarfs, she was rather frightened. The dwarfs, however, spoke kindly to her and when she told them her sad tale they were full of pity for her.

"If you will look after us," they said, "you can live here and we shall take care of you."

However, the dwarfs gave Snow White a warning. "We are out all day, working. If your stepmother learns that you are here, she may try to do you harm. So be sure to let no one into the house."

Snow White promised to be careful.

Meanwhile the Queen believed Snow White to be dead. So it was some time before she asked her magic mirror,

"Mirror, mirror, on the wall, who is the fairest of them all?"

She could not believe her ears when she heard this reply:

"Snow White is living still, and though thou, my Queen, art certainly fair, this child's great beauty doth make her more fair."

Great was the Queen's anger when she heard these words. She determined to find Snow White and kill her herself.

The Queen disguised herself as an old pedlar-woman. Then she travelled to the dwarfs' cottage, knocked on the door and shouted, "Laces and ribbons for sale!"

"What harm can this poor old woman do to me?" thought Snow White. She opened the door and chose some pretty pink laces for her corset. The old woman offered to lace up Snow White's corset for her. Snow White, suspecting nothing, agreed.

The Queen laced Snow White so tightly that she could not breathe, and she fell to the floor as if she were dead.

The dwarfs were shocked to find their beloved Snow White lying on the floor. When they saw how tightly she was laced, they cut the new laces. Soon she began to breathe again and gradually the colour returned to her cheeks.

The dwarfs were convinced that the old pedlar-woman must have been Snow White's wicked stepmother. They again warned Snow White to take great care.

The Queen hurried back through the forest filled with joy. When she reached the palace she went straight to her magic mirror.

When the Queen asked the usual question, the mirror replied,

"Snow White is living still, and though thou, my Queen, art certainly fair, this child's great beauty doth make her more fair."

The Queen was enraged. She prepared a poisoned comb, disguised herself and travelled to the dwarfs' cottage. She knocked on the door and shouted, "Pretty things to sell!"

Snow White put her head out of the window. "I have promised to open the door to no one."

"Never mind! You can look," replied the Queen, holding up the dainty comb.

Snow White could not resist it and she opened the door.

"You must let me comb your hair properly for you," the old woman said. The Queen then stuck the comb sharply into Snow White's head so that the poison went into her blood. She fell to the floor, as if dead.

When the seven dwarfs found Snow White lying on the floor, they suspected that her stepmother had been again. They soon found the poisoned comb and pulled it out.

Once more they begged Snow White never to open the door while they were out.

Later the jubilant Queen asked her mirror,

"Mirror, mirror, on the wall, who is the fairest of them all?"

Just as before, the mirror replied,

"Snow White is living still,
and though thou, my Queen,
art certainly fair, this child's great
beauty doth make her more fair."

At these words the Queen stamped her feet and beat on the mirror in her rage. "Snow White shall die," she vowed, "even if it costs me my life!"

The Queen knew that it might prove impossible to persuade Snow White to let her into the cottage a third time, so she plotted cunningly.

She took a lovely apple which had one green cheek and one rosy cheek. Then she put poison into the red cheek of the apple, leaving the green side free of poison. This time, she filled her basket with apples and disguised herself as a farmer's wife.

For the third time, she made her way to the dwarfs' cottage and knocked on the door.

"I am forbidden to open the door to anyone," said Snow White.

"I only want to get rid of these apples," replied the farmer's wife.

"I dare not take one," replied Snow White, shaking her head.

"Are you afraid that it's poisoned?" joked the farmer's wife. "Look, I'll cut it in two and we shall each eat half."

She held out the poisoned rosy half of the apple to Snow White and bit into the green half herself.

When Snow White saw the woman happily eating one half of the apple, she took the rosy half of the apple and bit into it. No sooner had she done so than she fell down dead.

The Queen laughed a horrible laugh. When she returned to her palace, at long last her mirror said,

"Thou, my Queen, art the fairest of them all!"

The jealous Queen was finally content.

When the dwarfs returned home in the evening, there lay Snow White on the floor, no longer breathing. They unlaced her corset, combed her hair and washed her face, and yet they could not revive her.

The dwarfs were heartbroken. They knew they must bury their beloved Snow White but they could not bear to do so.

The dwarfs had a glass coffin made, in order that they might still see Snow White. Then they each took it in turn to sit by the coffin, day and night.

There Snow White lay, as if still alive, but sleeping, with her skin as white as snow, her cheeks as red as blood and her hair as black as ebony. Even the birds came and wept to see her lying so still.

One day, it happened that a prince found the glass coffin. He fell in love with the beautiful girl inside.

"Let me have the coffin," he begged the dwarfs, "and I will give you whatever you ask."

But they only answered, "We would not part with Snow White for all the gold in the world."

"If you will give her to me," pleaded the Prince, "I shall cherish her all my life."

At length, the dwarfs took pity on the Prince and agreed to give him the coffin.

As the Prince's servants were carrying the coffin down the mountainside, they stumbled on the roots of a tree. The coffin was so badly jolted that the piece of apple, which had stuck in Snow White's throat, was flung out. She opened her eyes, lifted up the lid of the coffin and sat up.

The Prince was overjoyed to see her alive. "Come with me to my father's palace and we shall be married," he begged. Snow White agreed, for she had fallen in love with him instantly.

She said goodbye to the dwarfs who had loved her so dearly. Although they were sad to lose her, they knew that she would be happy.

It happened that Snow White's stepmother was among those invited to Snow White's wedding. Dressed in her finery, she stood before her mirror and asked,

"Mirror, mirror, on the wall, who is the fairest of them all?"

The mirror replied,

"The truth I must speak and I vow, that the young bride-to-be is more lovely than thou!"

The angry Queen felt that she must see this beauty. When she arrived at the feast and saw Snow White, her rage was so great that she fell down and died instantly.

And Snow White and the Prince lived in peace and happiness.